For my beloved mother, who introduced me
to Selma Lagerlöf's books. —Maja Dusíková

First published in the United States, Great Britain, Canada, Australia, and New Zealand
in 2014 by NorthSouth Books Inc., an imprint of NordSüd Verlag AG, CH-8005 Zürich, Switzerland.

Distributed in the United States by NorthSouth Books Inc., New York 10016.
Library of Congress Cataloging-in-Publication Data is available.
Printed in Germany by Grafisches Centrum Cuno GmbH & Co. KG, Calbe, August 2014.

ISBN: 978-0-7358-4190-1
1 3 5 7 9 • 10 8 6 4 2
www.northsouth.com

What the Shepherd Saw

Selma Lagerlöf • Maja Dusíková

NorthSouth

There was a man who went out in the dark night to borrow live coals to kindle a fire. He went from hut to hut and knocked. "Dear friends, help me!" he said. "My wife has just given birth to a child, and I must make a fire to warm her and the little one."

But it was way in the night, and all the people were asleep. No one replied.

The man walked and walked. At last he saw the
gleam of a fire a long way off. He went in that direction
and saw that the fire was burning in the open. A lot
of sheep were sleeping around the fire, and an old
shepherd sat and watched over the flock.

When the man who wanted to borrow fire came up to the sheep, he saw that three big dogs lay asleep at the shepherd's feet. All three awoke when the man approached and opened their great jaws, as though they wanted to bark; but not a sound was heard. The man noticed that the hair on their backs stood up and that their sharp white teeth glistened in the firelight. They dashed toward him.

He saw that one of the dogs bit at his leg, another at this hand, and the third clung to this throat. But their jaws and teeth wouldn't obey them, and the man didn't suffer the least harm.

Now, the man wished to go farther to get what he needed. But the sheep lay back-to-back and so close to one another that he couldn't pass them. So the man stepped upon their backs and walked over them to the fire. And not one of the animals awoke or moved.

When the man had almost reached the fire, the shepherd looked up. He was a surly old man who was unfriendly and harsh toward other human beings. And when he saw the strange man coming, he seized the long, spiked staff, which he always held in his hand when he tended his flock, and threw it at him. The staff came right toward the man, but, before it reached him, it turned off to one side and whizzed past him, far out in the meadow.

The man came up to the shepherd and said, "Good man, help me, and lend me a little fire! My wife has just given birth to a child, and I must make a fire to warm her and the little one."

The shepherd would rather have said no, but when he pondered that the dogs couldn't hurt the man, and the sheep had not run from him, and the staff had not wished to strike him, he was a little afraid and dared not deny the man that which he asked.

"Take as much as you need!" he said to the man.

By then the fire was nearly burnt out. There were no logs or branches left, only a big heap of live coals, and the stranger had neither spade nor shovel wherein he could carry the red-hot coals.

When the shepherd saw this, he said again, "Take as much as you need!" And he was glad that the man wouldn't be able to take away any coals.

But the man stopped and picked coals from the ashes with his bare hands and laid them in his mantle. And he didn't burn his hands when he touched them, nor did the coals scorch his mantle. He carried them away as if they had been nuts or apples.

And when the shepherd, who was such a cruel and hardhearted man, saw all this, he began to wonder to himself. What kind of a night is this, when the dogs do not bite, the sheep are not scared, the staff does not kill, nor the fire scorch? He called the stranger back and said, "What kind of a night is this? And how does it happen that all things show you compassion?"

Then the man said, "I cannot tell you if you yourself do not see it." And he wished to go his way, that he might soon make a fire and warm his wife and child.

But the shepherd did not wish to lose sight of the man before he had found out what all this might portend. He got up and followed the man till they came to the place where he lived.

Then the shepherd saw the man didn't have so much as a hut to dwell in, but that his wife and babe were lying in a mountain grotto where there was nothing except the cold, naked stone walls.

The shepherd thought that perhaps the poor, innocent child might freeze to death there in the grotto; and, although he was a hard man, he was touched and thought he would like to help the babe. So he loosened the knapsack from his shoulder, took from it a soft white sheepskin, gave it to the strange man, and said that he should let the child sleep on it.

Just as soon as he showed that he, too, could be merciful, his eyes were opened, and he saw what he had not been able to see before and heard what he could not have heard before.

He saw that all around him stood a ring of little silver-winged angels, and each held a stringed instrument, and all sang in loud tones that tonight the Savior was born who should redeem the world from its sins.

Then he understood how all things were so happy this night that they didn't want to do anything wrong.

And it was not only around the shepherd that there were angels, but they were everywhere. They sat inside the grotto, they sat outside on the mountain, and they flew under the heavens. They came marching in great companies, and, as they passed, they paused and cast a glance at the child.

There was such jubilation and such gladness and songs and play! And all this the shepherd saw in the dark night, whereas before he could not have made out anything. He was so happy his eyes had been opened that he fell upon his knees and thanked God.

What that shepherd saw, we might also see, for the angels fly down from heaven every Christmas Eve—if we could only see them.

You must remember this, for it is as true, as true as that I see you and you see me. It is not revealed by the light of lamps or candles, and it does not depend upon sun and moon; but that which is needful is that we have such eyes as can see God's glory.